For Sister Mary Ultan
- D.C.

For the memory of Margaret
- B.O'D.

For Joe, Bosun, and that little butterfly guy too
- K.B.

First published in Ireland by Discovery Publications, Brookfield Business Centre,
333 Crumlin Road, Belfast BT14 7EA
Telephone: 028 9049 2410
Email address: declan.carville@ntlworld.com

Text © 2001 Declan Carville

Book Design © 2001 Bernard O'Donnell

Illustrations © 2001 Kieron Black

A CIP catalogue record of this book is available from the British Library.

Printed in Belgium by Proost NV. Turnhout.

ISBN 0-9538222-2-2

1 2 3 4 5 6 7 8 9 10

The Incredible Sister Bridget

Declan Carville

illustrated by Kieron Black

book design by Bernard O'Donnell

Sister Bridget
was a very
good nun.

All the children loved her.

But it wasn't
because she
was such a
good teacher.

It had nothing to do with her giving them a little bit extra.

Oh, no.
The reason why everyone loved
Sister Bridget was because whenever
they went away for the day, she went
MAD!!!

She was always full of beans
first thing in the morning.

In fact Sister Bridget
never seemed to get tired.

She just
loved the
outdoors.

And never
felt the cold.

Sister Bridget loved all kinds of sports.

And was a great team leader.

She loved to play
the old games.

But she was a very modern nun as well.

She had loads of energy.

To the very end.

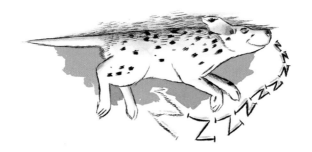